Russell Hoban

ACE DRAGON LTD

Pictures by Quentin Blake

JONATHAN CAPE
THIRTY BEDFORD SQUARE   LONDON

also by Russell Hoban and Quentin Blake

HOW TOM BEAT CAPTAIN NAJORK AND HIS HIRED SPORTSMEN
(Joint Winner of the Whitbread Award in 1974)

A NEAR THING FOR CAPTAIN NAJORK

THE TWENTY ELEPHANT RESTAURANT

**To Jake and Ben and Wieland,
dragon aces all**

First published 1980
Reprinted 1983
Text © 1980 by Russell Hoban
Illustrations © 1980 by Quentin Blake
Jonathan Cape Ltd, 30 Bedford Square, London WC1

British Library Cataloguing in Publication Data
Hoban, Russell
Ace Dragon Ltd.
I. Title II. Blake, Quentin
823'.9'1J   PZ7.H/
ISBN 0-224-01706-3

Printed in Great Britain by W. S. Cowell Ltd, Ipswich

John was walking down the street
when he heard something go Klonk.

John looked down and saw
a round iron plate in the pavement.
It was like a manhole cover.
On it he read: ACE DRAGON LTD.
John stamped three times on the iron cover.

A voice said, "Who is it?"
John said, "John."
The voice said, "What do you want?"
John said, "I want to know
what LTD means."

The voice said, "It means limited."
John said, "What does limited mean?"
The voice said, "It means I can't do
everything. I can only do some things."
John said, "What can you do?"

The voice said, "I can make fire come out of my nose and mouth. I can fly. I can spin gold into straw if you have any gold."

John said, "I don't have any gold."

The voice said, "Do you need any straw?"

John said, "No."

The voice said, "Then it doesn't matter. Do you want to go flying with me?"

John said, "Yes, I do."

The voice said, "Then you have to come down and fight me. If you win, I'll take you flying."

John said, "I can't lift this iron cover.
It's too heavy. Can you lift it?"
    The voice said, "No, I can't."
    John said, "How can we meet then?"
    The voice said, "Take the Underground
to Dragonham East. I'll meet you there."
    John said, "How shall I know you?"
    The voice said, "I'll be wearing
two pairs of wellingtons. How shall I
know you?"
    John said, "I'll have a sword."
    The voice said, "See you then."
    John said, "See you."

John took the Underground to
Dragonham East. There he saw
a dragon in wellingtons.

The dragon said, "How do you do?
I'm Ace Dragon Ltd."
John said, "How do you do? I'm John."

Ace and John found some waste ground
and got ready to fight.

Ace said, "Best out of three?"
John said, "Right."

Ace and John had their first fight.

John won.

Ace and John had their second fight.

John won.
John said, "That's two in a row.

That's best out of three. Now you have to take me flying."

John got on Ace's back and off they flew.

Ace and John flew very high and very far.
John said to Ace, "Can you do stunts?
Can you do sky-writing with fire?"

Ace did stunts and sky-writing with fire.

They were very high up
and it was getting dark when Ace said,
"I'm running out of petrol."

John said, "I didn't know you ran on
petrol."

Ace said, "That's how I make my fire
and that's what makes me go. I've used up
so much petrol with the sky-writing
that we haven't got enough to get us back."

John said, "Can't we glide back down
to earth?"

Ace said, "No, we can't.
If I stop flapping my wings we'll crash,
and it's a very long way down."

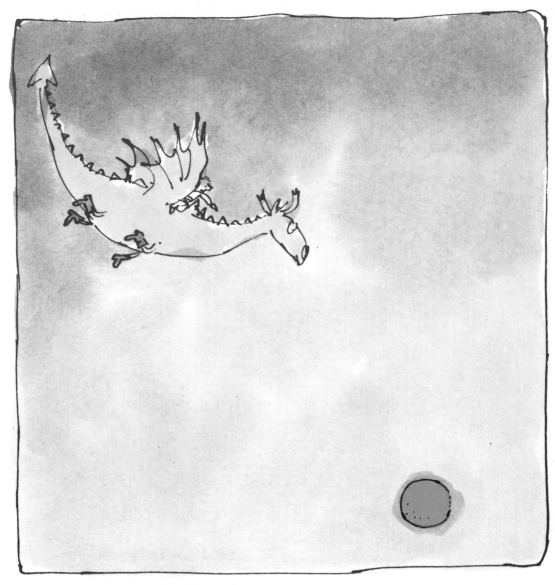

John said, "Look!
There's a little golden moon below us.
Can you get that far?"
　　Ace said, "I'll try."

They landed on the moon just as
Ace ran out of petrol.

John said, "We could jump back
down to earth if we had something soft
to land on."

Ace said, "Yes, but we *don't* have
something soft to land on."

John said, "This is a golden moon."
He sliced off some gold with his sword.
John said to Ace, "If you can spin gold
into straw you can make something soft
for us to land on."

Ace spun the gold into straw,
then John sliced off more gold
and Ace spun more straw.

Ace and John made
a great big bundle of straw.

Then they held on to the bundle
and they jumped.

Thump! They landed safely in the middle
of the waste ground.

Ace said, "I have to go home for supper now."
John said, "So do I. You know what, Ace?"
Ace said, "What?"
John said, "You're not so limited."

Ace said, "Thanks. I'll see you."
John said, "See you."
Then they both went home for supper.